STORE

DEPOT

TOY CONCEPT

Title: Toyland Express

Type: Wooden Train Set

Track Style: Interlocking

Cars: 6 Accessories: 39

TOYLAND EXPRESS

CAN YOU SEE WHAT I SEE?

TOYLAND EXPRESS

by Walter Wick

SCHOLASTIC INC.

New York   Toronto   London   Auckland
Sydney   Mexico City   New Delhi   Hong Kong

Published by Scholastic Inc.

SCHOLASTIC, CARTWHEEL BOOKS,

and associated logos are trademarks and/or

registered trademarks of Scholastic Inc.

ISBN 978-0-545-24483-1

10 9 8 7 6 5 4 3 2 1   11 12 13 14 15 16 17/0

Printed in the U.S.A. 87

First printing, September 2011

Book Design by Walter Wick and David Saylor

FOR ETHAN HELT

Library of Congress Cataloging-in-Publication Data

Wick, Walter.

Can you see what I see? : Toyland Express / by Walter Wick.   p. cm.

ISBN 978-0-545-24483-1

1. Picture puzzles – Juvenile literature. 2. Toys--Juvenile

literature.

GV1507.P47C355 2011

793.73--dc22   2010038596

CONTENTS

TOY MAKER'S WORKSHOP 11

FRESH PAINT 12

STORE WINDOW 14

HAPPY BIRTHDAY! 17

ALL ABOARD 18

MOUNTAIN PASS 20

AT THE CIRCUS 22

THE PASSING TRAIN 25

FORGOTTEN 26

YARD SALE 28

IN FOR REPAIRS 31

TOYLAND 32

ABOUT THIS BOOK 34

ABOUT THE AUTHOR 35

Can you see
what I see?
2 bells, a birdhouse,
a pencil, a pail,
a ball of string,
a long cat tail,
a baseball bat,
a leaf, 2 trees,
a broom, a brush,
a spring, 3 keys,
a bottle of glue,
a rubber band,
and a wooden train
that's made by hand!

Can you see
what I see?
4 elephants,
2 music men,
a bee, a bunny,
the number 10,
a rocking horse,
a polka-dot hat,
a frog, a flag,
a king, a cat,
a fire truck,
a fishing pole,
a TOYLAND engine
all set to roll!

Can you see
what I see?
A fiddling pig,
a juggling clown,
a ballerina's
silver crown,
a windup key,
2 cats, a kite,
a dog, a frog,
4 birds, a knight,
a hot-air balloon
upward bound,
and TOYLAND EXPRESS
going round and round!

Can you see
what I see?
An ice-cream sundae
with a cherry on top,
2 forks, a spoon,
a pink lollipop,
a rabbit, a rooster,
a little blue whale,
a pig, 3 ducks,
3 airplanes, a pail,
a half-eaten cupcake,
a striped balloon,
and musical notes
for a birthday tune!

Can you see
what I see?
A rocking horse,
a rolling hoop,
a birthday candle,
an ice-cream scoop,
a wheelbarrow,
a cat, a goose,
a green race car,
a red caboose,
a jack, 2 dice,
a hammer, a sword –
Now load the train,
it's time to board!

Can you see
what I see?
A sled, 3 skiers,
2 bunnies, 5 bears,
a mountain tunnel,
and snow-covered stairs,
a spoon, a pickax,
a fresh-cut tree,
a bottle of milk,
a shovel, a key,
a snowy owl,
a bright silver dime –
Now grab a blanket,
it's wintertime!

Can you see
what I see?
A flying trapeze,
a barrel of laughs,
3 camels, 2 zebras,
11 giraffes,
a baseball bat,
a bunch of balloons,
a hammer, a sword,
a band playing tunes,
a long-legged man
with top hat and cane –
Let's take a ride
on the circus train!

Can you see
what I see?
3 umbrellas,
a golden sun,
a fork, 5 bottles,
a hot dog bun,
4 dice, 2 mice,
a crayon, a cat,
a magic wand,
a red fire hat,
8 birds, a bunny,
a spaceship, a plane,
a spring, 3 clocks,
and a passing train.

Can you see
what I see?
A mousetrap, a magnet,
a feather, 4 keys,
a tennis racket,
and 2 TVs,
an acorn, a squirrel,
a bird that's pink,
a spider, 3 monkeys,
and a kitchen sink,
a pickup truck
with spots of rust,
and an old caboose
collecting dust.

Yard Sale

Can you see
what I see?
10 elephants,
2 fire trucks,
4 airplanes,
3 rubber ducks,
a record player,
a playing-card queen,
a thimble, a spool,
a sewing machine,
a basket, 4 bunnies,
a little pink dress,
and 3 lost wheels from
the TOYLAND EXPRESS!

Can you see
what I see?
Scissors, 5 crayons,
3 spools of thread,
a pencil, 4 buttons,
a wagon that's red,
a straw, a thumbtack,
a paper clip, too,
a red rubber band,
a bottle of glue,
a silver funnel,
a measuring cup,
and TOYLAND EXPRESS
getting all fixed up!

TOYLAND

Can you see

what I see?

5 ice-cream cones,

a hamburger bun,

a honey dipper,

and a golden sun,

10 bowling pins,

a dog, 5 ducks,

a whistle, 3 stop signs,

a limo, 4 trucks,

a pencil, a paintbrush,

a blue thumbtack, and

the TOYLAND EXPRESS

back on track!

As the youngest of four boys, I was often the happy recipient of hand-me-down toys. If a gender gap meant that my younger sister passed those toys by, I'm sure the best of them went on to another life. Where, I do not know. In my adult life I'm often on the hunt for props at flea markets and antique shops where I encounter such toys — faded, worn, and tattered. "Loved," as my wife, Linda, likes to say. But by whom, I do not know.

Can You See What I See?: Toyland Express, the eighth title in this search-and-find series, follows the life of a toy train from the workshop to the attic, only to be rescued at a yard sale and brought to life once again in a new home. As readers search for more than 250 hidden objects, it's my hope that they will also notice how the train takes on various transformations on its journey and how it's been modified and repurposed over time to adapt to new seasons, new trends, or new "owners" — just as it might if it were handed down to younger siblings or rescued by an enterprising child at a yard sale. But unlike my recent flea market finds, or the long-lost toys of my childhood, we need not wonder where the Toyland Express has been or where it might end up: That story is here for all to see — its "owner" is the reader holding this book.

Acknowledgments

While many of the props in the book have been acquired at flea markets, antique shops, toy stores, and online stores, the Toyland Express train featured throughout the book was built in my workshop by a team of artists, based on my original designs.

I would like to thank artist Randy Gilman for his contributions as lead model builder on the project. In addition to helping the train come to life, Randy built the circus tent and sideshow acts for "At the Circus," the dollhouse in "The Passing Train," the attic in "Forgotten," and numerous other ancillary props in the book. Thanks also to freelancer Andrew Mailhot for additional model making and his valuable assistance in the construction of the sets; to freelancer Bradley Wollman for further model making contributions; and to artist Michael Lokensgaard, who gave the Toyland Express train both its sparkling factory-paint finish and its convincing worn-out look. Michael also made the fun house for "At the Circus" and provided the art for the Toyland Express box top, box interior, and endpapers.

In addition, I would like to thank my wife, Linda Cheverton-Wick, for her ever-present support as my business manager and for her expert artistic advice on our many propping excursions in pursuit of the all-important toys that would help tell the story of the Toyland Express; our assistant Emily Cappa for her expert searches in the virtual world of the Internet and her tireless organizational skills in the real world of the studio; and Dan Helt, our longtime studio manager, who supervised the construction of all the sets, provided expert computer and camera assistance, managed the schedules of the freelance staff, and managed to witness the birth of his first child, Ethan, to whom this book is dedicated.

Finally, I would like to thank everyone at Scholastic, past and present, who have helped me realize the full potential of the Can You See What I See? series. In particular, I would like to thank editor Ken Geist and creative director David Saylor for their continued enthusiastic support, marketing director Julie Amitie for her ongoing efforts to promote the series, and president Ellie Berger for her vision and leadership.

—Walter Wick

All sets were designed, arranged, photographed, and digitally processed by the author. Spot illustrations were arranged by Randy Gilman and photographed by the author.

Walter Wick is the photographer of the I Spy series of books, with more than thirty-five million copies in print. He is author and photographer of *A Drop of Water: A Book of Science and Wonder*, which won the Boston Globe/Horn Book Award for Nonfiction, was named a Notable Children's Book by the American Library Association, and was selected as an Orbis Pictus Honor Book and a CBC/NSTA Outstanding Science Trade Book for Children. *Walter Wick's Optical Tricks*, a book of photographic illusions, was named a Best Illustrated Children's Book by the *New York Times Book Review*, was recognized as a Notable Children's Book by the American Library Association, and received many awards, including a Platinum Award from the Oppenheim Toy Portfolio, a Young Readers Award from *Scientific American*, a *Bulletin Blue Ribbon*, and a Parents' Choice Silver Honor.

Can You See What I See?, published in 2003, appeared on the *New York Times* Bestseller List for twenty-two weeks. His most recent books in the bestselling Can You See What I See? series are *Dream Machine*, *Cool Collections*, *The Night Before Christmas*, *Once Upon a Time*, *On a Scary Scary Night*, and *Treasure Ship*. Mr. Wick has invented photographic games for *GAMES* magazine and photographed covers for books and magazines, including *Newsweek*, *Discover*, and *Psychology Today*. A graduate of Paier College of Art, Mr. Wick lives in Connecticut with his wife, Linda.

More information about Walter Wick is available at
www.walterwick.com
and
www.scholastic.com/canyouseewhatisee/